SHAWNEEN AND THE GANDER

WEEKLY READER CHILDREN'S BOOK CLUB

INTERMEDIATE DIVISION

Books by Richard Bennett

NOT A TEENY WEENY WINK
SHAWNEEN AND THE GANDER
SKOOKUM AND SANDY

written and illustrated by Richard Bennett

Shawneen
and the Gander

DOUBLEDAY AND COMPANY, INC., GARDEN CITY, NEW YORK

SHAWNEEN AND THE GANDER

On the top of a high green hill in Ireland there
once lived a boy and his name was Shawneen.

One bright warm day while his mother was washing out the clothes, she said, "The fire is out and there
isn't a match in the house. Run down to Mrs. Murphy's
shop like a good lad and buy a box. Here is a penny."

Indeed there was no need for a second word about
that. Shawneen was always ready to go on errands to
Mrs. Murphy's.

"I will, to be sure," said he, putting his cap on his
head and the penny in his pocket.

Now at the foot of the hill there was a little village with a row of houses and shops up one side of the street and down the other.

Mrs. Murphy's was the prize of the lot. She sold everything.

If you wanted to buy a dress or if you wanted to buy a ham, Mrs. Murphy would be sure to have it.

When Shawneen arrived at her shop he was out of breath. He had been running down the hill, and it was a good way round when you came by the road.

Before opening the door, he stopped for a minute to look in the window.

The first shelf had the usual array of cups and saucers and the second shelf had nothing on it to talk about, but on the third shelf, right near the glass, Shawneen saw the most beautiful bugle he had ever seen in all his life.

It glistened so brightly in the sun that Shawneen could scarcely look at it.

It was all the color of gold and so shiny he could see himself seven times in it.

When Paddy the postman walked by the window to deliver the letters, seven Paddys walked by in the bugle. It was that bright.

12

Around the middle was tied a blue-and-yellow cord
with a silky tassel on each end as big as your hand.

Shawneen went into the shop.

"A box of matches, if you please, ma'am," said he to Mrs. Murphy; "and if it wouldn't be asking too much, may I have a toot on the bugle?"

"A toot, is it?" said Mrs. Murphy. "Indeed you may, my lad, two if you like. There is no harm in a good toot."

So Mrs. Murphy took the bugle out of the window and gave it to Shawneen. The end was cold and smooth and shaped so nicely that it fit snugly over his mouth.

"Now don't be afraid of it, my lad," said Mrs. Murphy. "Give us a good blow."

Shawneen blew very gently at first, then a little louder, and then so loud you could hear it down the street and over the hill and down by the sea.

Shawneen had never heard anything so fine in all his life.

"Ah, it's grand entirely," said he, stroking the tassels. "How much is it?"

"Ah, that's a very fine bugle," said Mrs. Murphy. "I couldn't let you have it for less than ten shillings and sixpence."

Shawneen blew on the bugle again but not so loud this time, then put it back on the counter.

Ten shillings and sixpence was a lot of money.

Indeed a pair of shoes would cost as much as that.

Shawneen gave Mrs. Murphy the penny and put the box of matches in his coat pocket.

He walked slowly out the door and down the street.

He was thinking very hard to himself. How could he get ten shillings and sixpence to buy the bugle in Mrs. Murphy's shopwindow?

There was no money at home to be spent for bugles. Indeed he was sure of that. Didn't his mother need a new shawl and the donkey a new harness and the window a new pane of glass? Wasn't his mother's tea-pot badly cracked and she often saying she wished she had the price of a new one? Weren't the soles of his own shoes so thin he decided to take a short cut across the fields as the gravel on the road hurt his feet?

"No, indeed," said Shawneen to himself, "it will be no use asking for ten shillings and sixpence to buy a bugle."

He jumped over the ditch and began to climb the hedge.

The heather and moss at the top felt nice and soft so he sat down for a bit to think the matter over.

He was no sooner nicely settled when all of a sudden he saw a strange little man, dressed all in green, asleep under a furze bush only a few feet away. He was no more than a foot long and his suit was so much the color of the grass about him that indeed Shawneen had to look sharp to make him out at all.

"It's a Leprechaun surely," whispered Shawneen to himself, "and the very lad who can tell me how I can get ten shillings and sixpence to buy the bugle."

Before you could say two two's, Shawneen had the little fellow about the waist.

Now you may be sure it isn't every day you see a Leprechaun and when you do you have to keep your eyes on him or it's off he is in no time at all.

Shawneen lifted the little maneen out from under the bush. The Leprechaun awoke with a great start and let such a yell out of him you wouldn't think he was equal to it. It was that loud.

18

"Ah, let me down now like a good lad," said the little fellow, kicking this way and that. "This is no way to be treating a gentleman."

"I will, faith," said Shawneen, "but first you must tell me how I can get ten shillings and sixpence to buy the bugle in Mrs. Murphy's shopwindow."

"Ah, that's easy enough," said the Leprechaun, "but you are hurting me now. Take your thumb off my stomach like a good lad."

Shawneen lifted his thumb a bit and then the Leprechaun began to stretch his arms and stretch his legs and rub his eyes at a great rate.

"This warm weather makes one very sleepy," said he.

"Never mind that now," said Shawneen; "how can I get ten shillings and sixpence to buy the bugle?"

"Ah, you are a very determined lad," said the Leprechaun. "Why, earn it, of course. You can't expect to get something for nothing."

"I know that well enough," said Shawneen, "but how can I earn all that money?"

The Leprechaun put one of his long bony fingers to the side of his nose and, leaning forward, whispered very mysteriously. "Not a word to a soul now," said he, "hatch the egg and sell the gander."

19

"What egg?" said Shawneen, squeezing the little fellow tighter than ever.

The Leprechaun didn't say another word but pointed to the earth.

20

Before Shawneen stopped to think, he glanced down
and there by the side of the ditch was the biggest goose
egg he had ever seen in all his life.

I needn't tell you the Leprechaun was gone in a flash.

"Well, the egg is real enough, faith," said Shawneen, picking it up and putting it in his cap to keep it from breaking.

"An egg the size of this should make a big gander and a big gander should bring a good price at the Fair. I should have enough money in all to buy my mother a new shawl and a new dress and a silver teapot and

have still enough left over to buy a bugle."

He was so excited he could hardly wait to get home.

The sooner the hatching began, the better.

Over the fields he went, leaping the ditches and climbing the hedges. That the egg wasn't broken was nothing less than a miracle.

When he reached home, his mother was hanging out the clothes.

"What have you there, my lad?" said she.

"A goose egg," said Shawneen.

"A goose egg, is it?" said his mother. "I have seen big eggs in my day but nothing the likes of that. Where did you find it?"

Now Shawneen remembered what the Leprechaun had said about keeping quiet.

"I was coming across the field," said he, "and there it was all by itself in the shelter of the ditch."

"And what will you do with an egg like that?" said his mother.

"Hatch it," said Shawneen. "Is there a hen setting?"

"There is, to be sure," said his mother. "Bring it into the shed."

She opened the henhouse door and pointed to a big brown hen nesting in one corner.

"I am afraid she will find it a bit uncomfortable," said Shawneen, pushing the hen aside a bit.

"Oh, in a few days she will be so used to it she will never know it was there at all," said his mother.

Now, goodness knows, the egg did make the poor hen sit a bit crooked, to be sure. But she was a quiet, obliging bird and went on sitting as if nothing had happened.

24

There she sat with one side up and one side down for days and days, a very mountain of patience.

Every morning Shawneen took a little peek under her wing to make sure all was going well and every now and then he went to have a look at the bugle in Mrs. Murphy's shopwindow. The bugle seemed to grow more beautiful every day and when Mrs. Murphy let him have a little toot on it now and then it sounded richer and sweeter as the days went by.

Well, the time passed as time will and soon the eggs were hatched—twelve yellow chicks and one yellow gosling. The chicks were fluffy and pretty as you may expect, but the gosling was a sight.

I don't think you could have found an uglier bird in the length and breadth of all Ireland.

His pinfeathers stuck out of him like the bristles of an old pig and his feet were so big and red and awkward he was forever stepping on his own toes.

His head was as big as a gosling twice his size and his poor little neck so thin and scrawny that it looked for all the world like a cabbage on the end of a broomstick.

"Ah, he is beautiful," said Shawneen to his mother; "may I raise him myself?"

"Indeed you may," said she. "I am sure I will have nothing to do with him. I have raised ducks and geese in my day but I have never seen anything come out of an egg the likes of that. Goodness knows what kind of a gander he will make. He has altogether too knowing a look in his eye, to my notion. Faith, he looks at you as if he knew what you are thinking. Take my word, the sooner you fatten him up and send him off to the Fair the better."

26

Shawneen thought this was a good idea. The sooner he had the money in his pocket, the sooner he could buy his bugle.

So every day he fed his gander the best of this and the best of that. Shawneen thought nothing was too good for him. In no time at all the gander was as big as the hens and as big as the turkeys and soon as big as the geese themselves.

Indeed he grew so fast he became the talk of all the neighbors for lands around.

"That's no common gander," everyone began to say. "He comes from no common stock, I can tell you. Look at the way he carries himself! You would think he owned the world and all!"

Now all this talk and all this attention made the gander very proud. Oh, you have no idea. In fact, he was so carried away with himself that he would have nothing to do with the other birds of the barnyard. With the air of a king he walked before them.

The ducks thought he was very funny and laughed at him.

The hens had never seen his like before and were a bit afraid of him.

But the geese were so put about with his fine airs they couldn't stand the sight of him.

Now with the animals it was a different story.

"Oh, he is only a gander," said they, and went on about their business. They wouldn't even look in his direction.

This didn't please the gander, you may be sure of that. Since they gave him no attention, he took great delight in teasing them every chance he could get.

Pulling the pigs' tails while they were eating supper was one of his favorite tricks.

"Faith, I will wring his neck if he goes on with any more of that," said Shawneen's father.

"Maybe he doesn't like curly tails," said Shawneen; "he was just trying to straighten them out a bit."

"Straighten them out, indeed," said his father. "I'll straighten him out in short order if he goes on with any more of that nonsense."

One day the gander made faces at the donkey and the poor little fellow was so frightened he backed the cart wheel over a boulder and upset two churns of milk and two fine baskets of eggs.

Another day he chased the goats over the young cabbages and the one little patch of potatoes. You can imagine the state of the garden.

One day Shawneen's mother decided to clean the house. She washed the windows and swept the floor and polished the pots and pans. When everything was nice and neat, she went out to get a pail of water.

Meanwhile, it started to rain. Over the half door flew the gander as easy as you please and made himself at home in front of the fireplace. He shook the rain off his feathers and flapped his wings, blowing the ashes and cinders all over the house.

"Oh, glory," said Shawneen's mother when she opened the door, "that bird will drive us out of house and home. I think the safest place for him is in the pot."

32

"Oh, no," said Shawneen, "he was just trying to be helpful and blow up the fire a bit. He is a very thoughtful gander."

"Thoughtful, indeed," said his mother. "It's a nice job he has given me with his thoughtfulness. Another trick like that and into the pot he goes."

I needn't tell you Shawneen was beginning to get worried when he heard this. The gander was acting very strange, to be sure. He would never get to the Fair at the rate he was going. But never a fear had the gander.

He made friends with all the hungry crows of the neighborhood and one evening invited them all in for supper. They ate up the grain in no time at all and the poor hens had to go to bed hungry. Oh, he was a holy terror.

There was no holding him.

Another day Shawneen's mother made some bread. She mixed the dough in a large pan and put it on the table near the fire while she hung out the clothes.

It was a warm afternoon and the gander was feeling a bit drowsy. He jumped over the half door again, as familiar as you please, and settled himself for a nice comfortable nap in the very middle of the pan.

34

"Oh, glory," said Shawneen's mother when she opened the door. "This is too much. Tomorrow is Fair day. That gander goes with your father. Whatever price he will bring he will have to go. We can't put up with him a minute longer. There is something very strange about that bird. Heaven knows what he may do to us all if he takes the notion."

"Sh, sh, sh, sh," said the gander, jumping out of the pan and leaping over the half door. He stood outside for a minute with his ear to the crack and heard the whole story. He knew very well that when ganders or geese went to the Fair they never came back. Oh, he was no fool.

That night he never slept a wink. He stood on one foot and then on the other. When the cock began to

crow, his mind was made up. He would hide outside
the garden wall until Shawneen's father was well out
of sight.

Now as luck would have it, who should be sleeping
outside the garden wall that very minute but Ned the
Napper—the foxiest rogue in all Ireland. He was forever sneaking up and down the countryside, stealing
everything he could lay his hands on.

Over the wall came the gander and landed squarely
on top of his head. Feathers went flying, I can tell you.
Such kicking and biting you never saw. For a while in

the dim light you couldn't tell which was Ned and which was the gander. But I am sorry to say foxy Ned soon had the upper hand. He tucked the gander safely in his bag, tossed it over his shoulder, and made off east the road.

That morning when Shawneen's father had hitched the donkey to the cart and was ready to be off, no gander could be found. They all looked high and they all looked low but no gander could they see. They looked behind this and they looked behind that, but not a feather of him was in sight.

"Well, gander or no gander," said Shawneen's father, "I can't wait any longer." So he slapped the lines over the donkey's back and set off to the Fair.

Shawneen watched the donkey cart rattling down the lane and through the gate. Soon it turned a bend of the road and was out of sight. He stood in the middle of the road, wondering what to do next. He had waited so long for the egg to hatch and for the gander to grow a bit. Indeed, it was a trial keeping him out of the pot with all his strange actions. Now when he was ready for the Fair he was nowhere to be found. Shawneen couldn't help but think of the bugle in Mrs. Murphy's shopwindow. It was likely to stay

just where it was. Shining away for itself on the top shelf.

Shawneen ate his breakfast very slowly, thinking very hard to himself.

"Perhaps he has gone for a walk," said he to his mother.

"Very likely, indeed," said she. "Faith, he was liable to do most anything."

Shawneen decided to take a walk east the road. The gander might have gone in that direction.

Now Shawneen hadn't gone very far when he met two women gathering their washing off the hedges where it had been put out to dry.

"Did you see a big gander pass by here, by any chance?" said Shawneen.

"A gander, is it?" said one of the women very crossly. "No, indeed, but I would like to get a glimpse of the rogue that made off with my husband's new Sunday shirt and my two fine linen aprons."

Shawneen went on a little further until he came to a little cottage. Outside the door was an old woman spinning.

"Did you see a big gander pass by here, by any chance?" said Shawneen.

"A gander, is it?" said the old woman. "No, my child, but I would like to get a glimpse of my little teapot I put out to dry on the window sill. A fine, shiny little teapot it was. The fairies must have had their eyes on it."

Shawneen went on his way. Around another bend of the road he met two men cutting turf.

"Did you see a big gander pass by here, by any chance?" said Shawneen.

"A gander, is it?" said one of the men very crossly. "Indeed I didn't, but I would like to lay my hands on the rogue that made off with our coats and dinner pail when our backs were turned."

A little way further Shawneen came to a tinkers' van that was standing by the side of the road. Three of the tinkers were talking together in a very wild manner.

"Did you see a big gander pass by here, by any chance?" asked Shawneen.

"A gander, is it?" said one of the tinkers very crossly. "No, I didn't, but I would like to lay my hands on the rogue that made off with our finest pots and pans."

Now a little way further Shawneen came to a cross-roads where some young people were dancing on a

large flat stone by the side of the ditch.

"Did you see a big gander pass by here, by any chance?" cried Shawneen.

The young people were so busy laughing and dancing and the fiddler so busy playing and calling out the sets that no one paid any attention.

44

Shawneen said no more but walked slowly along the little road that ran up the side of a hill.

"A flock of ganders could pass by that crowd and I am sure they would be none the wiser," said Shawneen to himself. "It's too busy dancing they are."

Now he hadn't gone many steps when he met two guards.

"Did you see a big gander pass by here, by any chance?" Said Shawneen.

"A gander, is it?" said one of the guards. "No, my lad, but we would like to lay our hands on Ned the Napper. We heard he was around these parts."

Shawneen sat on a stone nearby and wondered what to do next. His hopes of finding the gander seemed less than ever.

Now during all this time great clouds had been rolling across the sky and soon big raindrops began to fall.

"I'll be drenched surely," said Shawneen, looking about for a bit of shelter. An old ruined castle at the top of a nearby hill was the only thing in sight. He climbed over the hedge and ran up the hill. He walked quickly across the yard and through the castle door.

It was dark and gloomy among the old walls and the ivy rustled and whispered in the wind. In the far corner of the first room Shawneen found a spot that was fairly dry in spite of the wind and rain.

Now he was no sooner nicely settled when all of a sudden he heard a strange noise in the next room.

47

"Sh, sh, sh, sh," it went very softly.

"Sh, sh, sh, sh," it went again a little louder than before.

"Rain or no rain, I'll stay here no longer," said Shawneen, starting for the door.

"Sh, sh, sh, sh," came the noise again, a little louder this time.

Shawneen stopped a bit. He had heard that sound before.

He tiptoed gently to the door of the next room and peeked in. You can well imagine his surprise. There on the floor was a fierce-looking man fast asleep. By his side was a big bag—and what in the world should

48

be sticking out of the side of it but the gander's head.

The man stirred in his sleep. He began to rub his nose. He was going to wake up, there was no doubt about that. Shawneen held his breath.

Just then the gander leaned over and said, "Sh, sh," so softly in his ear the man went on sleeping as sound as ever.

Then the gander began to tear the sack very slowly with his strong bill.

As the hole became bigger and bigger, Shawneen suddenly remembered what the guards had said about Ned the Napper. Beyond a doubt this was the very lad the guards were after.

Without a word Shawneen tiptoed across the room. He ran out the door and down the hill.

His feet splashed in all the pools and the rain

blinded him so badly he could hardly see. As luck would have it, the guards hadn't gone very far. Shawneen came running up, puffing and blowing. He was so excited he could hardly speak.

"Up there, up there!" shouted Shawneen, pointing to the castle.

"What's up there, my lad?" said one of the guards.

"Ned the Napper, I think, sir," said Shawneen.

Without another word they all ran up the hill. Before you could say two two's, the guards had the fierce-looking man safely between them.

With a few good bites, the gander stepped out of the bag and gave himself a good shake. He was as cross as two sticks. And indeed it's well he may be. To be tossed into a bag like an old cabbage head would be hard on anyone's dignity.

"This is a lucky day for you, my lad," said one of the guards to Shawneen. "It will be well worth your while to come down to the barracks with us. This is Ned the Napper all right, all right. It's a long chase he has given us. We will leave his bag here and take care of that later. It will be quite safe in this deserted place."

So down the hill they went—foxy Ned with a guard on each arm and Shawneen and the gander out before.

A few minutes later Shawneen and one of the guards walked out of the barracks door. Shawneen was carrying a little leather sack in one hand. In it was enough

money to buy teapots and shoes and dresses and shawls. And bugles!

"Well indeed, my lad," said the guard; "you well deserve this reward for telling us about Ned the Napper. Now that the rain is over, let us go back to the castle and see what we can find in the bag."

So up the hill they went. When they reached the castle, the guard turned the bag upside down.

Coats and shirts and pots and pans came tumbling out on the floor.

"Why, this must be the old lady's teapot," said Shawneen, "all wrapped up in the turf cutter's coat,

and here are the women's aprons and the tinkers' pots and pans."

"Do you know who all these things belong to?" said the guard, scratching his head.

"Indeed I do," said Shawneen, rattling the money in the little sack. "It's scattered west the road they are —tinkers and turf cutters, old ones and young ones. Have a little patience now, your honor. I'll bring them all flying in short order."

Without another word he was down the hill and into Mrs. Murphy's shop. Before you could say two two's, he was out again and up the hill, blowing the fine shiny bugle for all he was worth. Ah, indeed, it's fine and clear it sounded, ringing out through all the countryside. Through all the lands around, its like was never heard before. All who heard it came running up the hill. The tinkers, the women, the turf cutters, the

dancers—even the old woman left her spinning wheel and came as far as she could to see what was making such a sweet sound. Soon they all arrived. Shawneen lined them up before the castle door. When each received his bit, Shawneen blew a fine lively toot on the bugle. Then there was merry talk, you may be sure.

59

A few minutes later they all went down the hill and west the road. The fiddler played and the young people sang and the gander strutted out before as if he owned the world and all.

"Oh, he is no common gander," everyone said. "It's easy to see that. There isn't a finer bird in the length and breadth of all Ireland."

ABOUT THE AUTHOR:

Richard Bennett was born in Ireland and came to this country at the age of four, when his parents bought a farm in the western part of Washington State. Most of their neighbors were Siwash Indians, and years later their activities provided Richard Bennett with the background for a number of books including *Skookum and Sandy*, a tale of a boy, his goat, and their Indian friends.

After graduating from the University of Washington, Mr. Bennett spent several years teaching art, perfecting his woodcut technique, and traveling in Europe. His early childhood and his visits to Ireland are recalled in SHAWNEEN AND THE GANDER, which captures the atmosphere of the Irish countryside and the delightful flavor of its folk humor.

Richard Bennett has illustrated many books other than his own, and his woodcuts have been displayed in libraries and museums. In between visits to Ireland, California, and Washington, Mr. Bennett lives in New York City.